D0602485

Oh My Gosh, Mrs. McNosh!

Oh My Gosh, Mrs. McNosh!

by Sarah Weeks

pictures by Nadine Bernard Westcott

LAURA GERINGER BOOKS
An Imprint of HarperCollinsPublishers

Oh My Gosh, Mrs. McNosh!

Text copyright © 2002 by Sarah Weeks

Illustrations copyright © 2002 by Nadine Bernard Westcott

Manufactured in China. All rights reserved.

For information address HarperCollins Children's Books,
a division of HarperCollins Publishers, 10 East 53rd Street,
New York, NY 10022.

www.harperchildrens.com

Library of Congress Cataloging-in-Publication Data

Weeks, Sarah.

    Oh my gosh, Mrs. McNosh! / by Sarah Weeks ; pictures by Nadine Bernard Westcott.

      p.   cm.

    Summary: Mrs. McNosh's dog breaks his leash and leads her on a merry chase in the park, disrupting a
boating party, a wedding, and a ball game.

    ISBN 0-694-01204-1

    [1. Dogs—Fiction. 2. Parks—Fiction. 3. Humorous stories. 4. Stories in rhyme.] I. Westcott, Nadine
Bernard, ill. II. Title.

PZ8.3.W4125 Oh 2002

[E]—dc21   2001024396

                                                         CIP

                                                         AC

Typography by Jennifer Crilly

10 11 12 13 SCP 20 19 18 17 16 15 14 13 12 11

❖

First Edition

For my country neighbors—

Malcolm, Vicky, Emery, and Rupert

—SW

To Ella and Stukely

—NBW

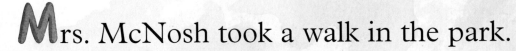

Mrs. McNosh took a walk in the park.

Her dog saw a squirrel and started to bark.

"Stop barking! Stop pulling!" said Nelly McNosh.

But George wouldn't listen, and so—

Oh, my gosh!

He zipped through the flowers
and skipped through the trees,
barking at bicycles, babies, and bees.

He dove and he wove right past Mrs. McNosh.

"I'll catch you!" cried Nelly.

But then—

The boat sprang a leak,

so George had to jump out.

"I'll catch you!" cried Nelly.

She caught . . .

a big trout.

He crashed through a wedding
and trashed the buffet.
"I'll catch you!" cried Nelly.
She caught . . .

the bouquet.

"Come back here right now," hollered Mrs. McNosh.
But George just kept running until—

Oh, my gosh!

He bumped the plump umpire,
then jumped the stone wall.
"I'll catch you!" cried Nelly.
She caught . . .

a fly ball.

He danced and he pranced,

then he shook and he rolled.

"I'll catch you!" cried Nelly.

She caught . . .

a bad cold.

"That's it, I give up. I can't catch you, it's true.

I know when I'm licked.

I've been licked, George, by you."

So Nelly walked back to her house all alone,
and there on the porch she saw George's old bone.
"I wish he'd come back," sniffled Mrs. McNosh.
Then she opened the door and she cried—